Ben is in kin

He will be in first grade soon.

KINDERGARTEN KIDS

On Our Way to First Grade

by Kate Howard
illustrated by Mike Byrne

Scholastic Inc.

No part of this publication may be reproduced, stored in a retrieval system, or transmitted in any form or by any means, electronic, mechanical, photocopying, recording, or otherwise, without written permission of the publisher. For information regarding permission, write to Scholastic Inc., Attention: Permissions Department, 557 Broadway, New York, NY 10012.

ISBN 978-0-545-82340-1

Text copyright © 2015 by Kate Howard
Illustrations copyright © 2015 by Mike Byrne

Published by Scholastic Inc. SCHOLASTIC and associated logos are trademarks and/or registered trademarks of Scholastic Inc.

19 18 21/0

Printed in the U.S.A. 40

First printing, May 2015

Ben is sad.
He will miss his kindergarten friends.

"Today is the last day of kindergarten," says Ms. Green. "No!" Ben says.

"What is wrong, Ben?" asks
Ms. Green.
"I do not want to go to first grade,"
Ben says.
"I will miss you."

"I will miss you, too."
Ms. Green smiles.
"But you will love first grade."

Ben is not sure.
What if first grade is hard?

Ben helps Emma put away books.
"Will we read books in first grade?" asks Ben.

"You will read lots of books in first grade," says Ms. Green. "Fun new books about sharks and pirates!"

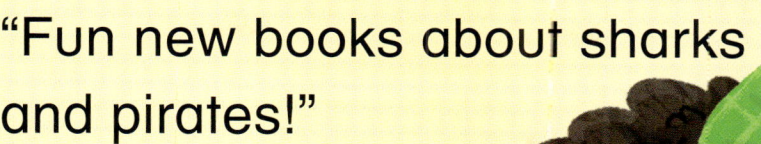

Ben and Jack clean the art table. "Will we do art in first grade?" asks Ben.

"Yes, you will do art in first grade," says Ms. Green.
"Fun new projects with clay and paint."

"Will we eat lunch in first grade?" asks Ben.

"Yes, you will eat lunch in first grade," says Ms. Green. "New foods and yummy old foods, too."

Ben and Gavin take pictures off the window.
"Will we play outside in first grade?" asks Ben.

"Yes, you will play outside in first grade," says Ms. Green. "Fun new games like soccer and kickball."

Ben looks at his friends.
"Will there be friends in first grade?"

"There will be friends in first grade," says Ms. Green.
"New friends and old friends, too!"

Last fall, Ben was worried about kindergarten.

Now he knows kindergarten is super.
Maybe first grade will be super, too.

"Kids, we had a great year," says Ms. Green.

"Now you are ready for first grade. But first it is time for our kindergarten party."

"A party?" says Ben.
Ben loves parties.

"Will we have a party like this in first grade?" he asks.

"Yes, you will have parties in first grade," says Ms. Green. "But this is a special party. It only happens in kindergarten."

Ben is curious.
What is so special about this party?

"This is your Stepping Up party," says Ms. Green.
"You will walk across the bridge to first grade."

Ben walks across the rainbow bridge.
His friends cheer.

Then the class sings a special song.

Ben is happy.
He learned a lot in kindergarten.

And now he knows he will learn even more in first grade!